The Son
of the
Leopard

The Son of the Leopard

by Harold Courlander

Woodcuts by Rocco Negri

Crown Publishers, Inc.
New York

For Adelaide

The Prophecy

"Though these shells be cast a thousand times on the ground and seem to fall differently, for each man they can tell only one story, and that is his story. Each man suffers his destiny, whether he speaks or is silent, whether he rides or walks. Three times you will fail. The first time you will fail through vanity. The second time you will fail through weakness. The third time you will fail through strength. And at last you will succeed through sorrow."

TODAY there are only broken stone walls atop the mountain called Aini, and these are all that are left of the village of Adi Keritoha. The mountain once had many trees, and in the village were many houses of stone, but the trees have disappeared, the houses have been washed away by rain and wind, and there is not a single living soul in Adi Keritoha.

All that is remembered of the people of Adi Keritoha is in the legend of Wolde Nebri, whose name means the Son of the Leopard. For it was their destiny to build the village out of the stone of the mountainside, grow wheat and durra in the valley below, raise children one generation following another, and finally be scattered and lost in the flow of time.

Of the people of that village, only a few are ever recalled, and they are the ones who are part of the legend of Wolde Nebri.

1

It is told that the people of Adi Keritoha came from the South and drove away the people who lived around the mountain of Aini. They then built the village far above the valley, on a precipice which overlooked the horizon on three sides—the East, the West, and the North. For a reason never mentioned among them, they turned their backs on the South. The pathways down the mountainside pointed to the East and North and West, but there were no trails leading in the direction from which they had come. In Wolde Nebri's day there were more than five hundred families in Adi Keritoha.

So the old people say.

When Wolde Nebri was born there was a seven-day ceremony to establish the identity of his soul. For it was believed that every living person had lived before in another age. A child who came into the world on the mountain of Aini was not a being born for the first time. He was a continuation of an earlier life. When a man died he was destined to come back again in a future year.

The Head Man of Adi Keritoha had ruled since the first week of his life. When he was born it was determined that he was the ancient Head Man Mogaws, returned again to the living. So he was given his rightful name, Mogaws, and the Head Man then ruling Adi Keritoha was deposed and sent out into the desert to die. Mogaws' word was law even before he could speak. The Holy Men of Adi Keritoha would gather in a cave in the mountain and sing and beat drums till one of them achieved a state of ecstasy, and in this state he would then go out of the cave and issue Mogaws' decrees, and the people would obey. When Mogaws was old enough to talk, the Holy Men no longer spoke for him.

So it was with every man, woman, and child in Adi Keritoha. Each man's name, his work, and his fate were predetermined by the life he had lived long ago. The Holy Men had all been Holy Men before. The iron-smith was an ironsmith because he had been a famous maker of spears and knives in times past.

The knowledge of this continuing life was a comfort and a fear. There was no ending. The arts of medicine, metalwork, and war could never be lost, for those who gained the knowledge would return with that knowl-edge after death. But hatred, injustice, and wickedness also lived in this way from generation to generation.

When Wolde Nebri was born the Holy Men went to the mountain cave and played their drums and sang and danced to determine his rightful place in the village. The first day of the ceremony passed without any reve-lation. None of the Holy Men achieved an ecstatic state. So went the second day, and the third and the

fourth. They fasted and drank only water, because that was the law. The fifth and sixth day passed, and their drumming and singing echoed among the mountain passes. And at midnight on the seventh day one of the Holy Men leaped up with a wild cry and flung himself first on one person and then another, biting them with his teeth. They calmed him, and when he was quiet he lay as though dead upon the ground. When he spoke he said: "The child is the Son of the Leopard."

They went to the parents of the child and said: "His name is Wolde Nebri, he is the Son of the Leopard."

Word then went through the village that Wolde Nebri had returned, and people went inside their houses and closed the doors. In the marketplace the next day they said to one another: "Have you heard? Wolde Nebri has come back."

No child was born in Adi Keritoha but what men would ask themselves questions as to their role in the matter. Each man would ask himself: "When I lived before, was it in the time of the One Who Has Returned? Did I owe him money? Did we have cruel words? Does he cherish or hate me?"

With many a newborn child it would not matter. He was perhaps merely a returning obscure farmer or hunter, or a Holy Man or a metalsmith. But in the case of Wolde Nebri it mattered greatly.

For after four hundred and seventy-eight years,

Wolde Nebri had found them, after they had destroyed him in the South. Eight years he had been their chief, and in those eight years he had slaughtered more than a thousand men and ruled them under a cloud of terror. At last they had turned upon him and burned him alive in his house. Afterwards they had lived in great fear of the day he would return to avenge himself. Finally they had agreed among themselves to go away from their country to an inaccessible place Wolde Nebri would never be able to find. And so they had gone northward, through desert and mountains, walking each day, stopping only to sleep and tend the sick. They had carried the infants and infirm upon their backs. Some had died of thirst, others of hunger. Two seasons they had stopped in fertile valleys to plant grain to feed them on the march. In the seventh month of the fourth year they had come upon the mountain of Aini, and here they had settled and founded the village of Adi Keritoha. There were trails only to the North, the East, and the West, and only desolate wastes to the South. Four hundred and seventy-eight years they had lived there on the mountain, and they had all but forgotten.

And now, once again, the Son of the Leopard was among them.

The Head Man Mogaws called the elders of the village to a meeting to discuss the event. Among them were Shitol, the maker of weapons; Ketap, the maker of charms and fetishes; Awm, the maker of bows and arrows, though in this present life he made no bows and arrows because they were no longer used; Nauti, the maker of plows; and Nahasi, the bronze caster.

Mogaws said: "Four hundred and seventy-eight years we have been free of the terror of Wolde Nebri. Long must he have searched for us. Great must be his anger, first that we destroyed him, then that we abandoned our town and fled from him. What shall we do now?"

Awm, the maker of bows and arrows, said: "In my previous state of existence I was not of his generation. He cannot be angry with me. It isn't my concern."

Shitol, the maker of swords and knives, said then: "I was of the generation before Wolde Nebri, but my son was alive in his day. How can I tell if my son was in favor with him or not?"

Ketap the maker of fetishes said: "I was alive in the time of Wolde Nebri, until his soldiers came upon my house and slaughtered me with my wife and children."

Nahasi the bronze caster said: "I know not if I was there."

And Nauti the maker of plows said: "What does it

matter if we were there? Wolde Nebri showed no discrimination. He killed when he wished and destroyed when the fancy overtook him. He is here."

Then Mogaws the Head Man asked: "Is it possible that the Son of the Leopard may have mellowed since that time? Perhaps it will no longer be the same as it was."

Nauti the maker of plows replied: "Perhaps it is so. But who will ever know for certain until he feels the blade of Wolde Nebri's spear in his stomach?"

The elders talked this way, back and forth, recalling the past and guessing at the future. At last the Head Man said:

"Wolde Nebri was not Head Man of the village, but chief of the countryside. He scorns my humble place in life, so my position is not in question. There are none in Adi Keritoha who were his servants or soldiers. So for the moment there is no danger."

The weapons maker said: "Perhaps it is so. But if we destroy him now we might go our way without fear."

The bronze caster said: "Perhaps it is so. Yet would his wrath not be even greater if we destroyed him a second time?"

The plowmaker said: "Are we prepared then to abandon Adi Keritoha and find another site? Where would we go?"

The Head Man said: "There is no hurry. Let us wait and watch. While he is so young he cannot get out of hand. This is my decision."

Wolde Nebri drank from the breast of his mother and grew strong. She carried him in the sling on her back when she went to cut grain in the fields, and when she ground meal in the house he played upon the floor. His father, Tchimara the hunter, played with Wolde Nebri at night near the fire, though his heart was heavy. It was his fate to be the father of the Son of the Leopard, and it was also his fate to love his child, and the two things tormented him so that his eyes sank deeper in his head and he never smiled. When Wolde Nebri crawled to his father's lap and grasped him by the finger, Tchimara looked and asked himself: "Is this small hand the one which bloodied a thousand spears? How can it be?" And when he killed a gazelle he would ask himself: "This is for the little helpless one, but will it nourish him for the hour he awaits to avenge himself?" This is the way it was with Tchimara the hunter, until one day he was slain by a lion. Then it was Kohop, Wolde Nebri's mother, who played with him at night before the fire. Kohop too asked herself questions: "Can this really be the Son of the Leopard? Oh, I do not care! I do not care!" Though she did not care, the questions came again and again. One day Wolde Nebri, crawling upon the ground, came upon a sharp knife and took it in his small hands and studied it. Kohop dropped her grinding stone in fear. She snatched the knife away and hurled it into the water jar.

In the marketplace where Kohop sold the grain from the fields, Wolde Nebri crawled on the ground among the pots and figs. If other small children picked a fruit from a pile, the owner would shout and drive them away. If Wolde Nebri did the same, they watched in silence. If he sat on the earth and looked a man in the face, that man would turn his eyes elsewhere in embarrassment.

When Wolde Nebri approached other infants, their mothers would snatch them away, saying not what was in their minds but perhaps: "You bad disobedient one! Come out of the sun, lest the shadow of a demon fall on you!"

Thus the years went by. When Wolde Nebri was six, he herded his mother's goats, driving them down from the mountain village each morning, watching them graze among the grass and shrubs, and driving them back at nightfall. When he was thirsty during the hot day he took milk from the goats. Sometimes he found figs or cactus fruits growing among the rocks, and these he ate. When Wolde Nebri's herd approached, other small boys drove their own goats farther down the mountainside. When Wolde Nebri's goats came to a watering place dug in the bottom of a dry riverbed, the other goatherds drove their own animals away and waited at a distance.

If Kohop were alone she was as welcome, no more no less, as she had used to be, for she was not held responsible. No one was responsible for the souls he unwittingly helped to return to life. But in the company of Wolde Nebri, other women seemed unaware of Kohop's presence.

Growing up in the midst of swarming human life, Wolde Nebri heard many voices, but they spoke rarely to him. And when they did, the words were dry, and did not quench his thirst.

When Wolde Nebri was ten he understood that except for Kohop he was alone. Why that should be, he did not understand. Once he came upon children playing on the trail below the village, and said: "I will play this game also." But they moved aside and stood waiting for him to go his way. A fury took hold of him, and he ran at them screaming and throwing stones. They fled into the village, and when he arrived there the place was quiet. No one in the streets, and the doors of the houses were closed.

One day Kohop became sick, and though the herb doctor came and prepared medicines for her, she soon died. She was taken to the top of the mountain by the Holy Men, and her body was covered with stones. On the top of the stones a knife was planted, its blade pointing upward so that a demon might not alight there.

Wolde Nebri had the silent house to himself then, and he talked only to his goats. At night he dreamed: "I will play this game also."

Mogaws the Head Man listened to the tales about Wolde Nebri: The Son of the Leopard went here, he went there, he hurled a stone at a house, he kicked dust in the face of the bronze caster's son, he spat on Mogaws' own door, he set fire to the carpenter's straw-stack. The elders said: "We must do something now, he is growing strong and angry." But Mogaws cast his eyes on the ground and clicked his tongue. "Not yet, there is no solution yet." The Holy Men went to the mountain cave to seek a solution, but there were no revelations.

Then one day Wolde Nebri dragged some carrion into the holy mountain cave, so that hyenas, eager to eat, entered the cave and defiled it. He removed the knives from atop the stone graves on the mountain, so that the demons might alight there. And he rolled boulders down into the village, wounding a blind weaver sitting before his house.

Mogaws met again with the elders and said: "Very well. Now we must do something. Let us drive him away."

And that night when Wolde Nebri returned to Adi Keritoha with his goats, the people of the village blocked the trail and hurled stones at him, shouting: "Go whence you came! Go whence you came!"

Bleeding from his wounds, the Son of the Leopard ran in terror down the trail that went to the West. He slept without blanket or fire under an overhanging rock, and when day came he went again with the trail that descended to the West. He felt his heart beating within him, and said to himself: "I have one friend. The heart that beats within me is my friend. To him only will I talk."

Wolde Nebri grew into manhood, but he wandered through the land as one without a country. He carried on his back the long broadsword of the plains, and walked with pride like a warrior. He rested nowhere for long, but went his way. To those who greeted him with the word "Peace," he replied: "Peace, but there is no peace." And to those who asked his name he replied:

"I am he who carries the broadsword." And when men asked where he came from, Wolde Nebri said: "Is not this the great mystery of life?" And whoever asked, "What do you seek?" would hear him reply: "I know not."

He went through the country of the Baria, the Beni Amer, and the Mensa. He went through the country of the Habab, the Cunama, and the Tacrura. He went through the country of the Ad Temariam, the Hanendoa, and the Bora.

And in the land of the Bora he came upon a deep well, surrounded by Bora warriors sharpening their knives and their spears. He asked for water, and they permitted him to drink. Then they asked where he came from, and where he was going, and he asked them in turn how were their homes and their cattle, and why they were preparing their spears. And they replied:

"The Halhal are stealing our cattle and wish to drive us away from the wells. One thousand cows have they stolen, and of our men they have already killed five hundred."

They gave Wolde Nebri bread and milk, and he sat among them and listened to their account of the depredations of the Halhal. When the story was finished he said:

"Today count me as one of the Bora. Let us fight the Halhal."

And they replied to him: "Each month we have fought them, and each month our numbers shrink, while the Halhal grow rich and fat. What then shall we do?"

"Let us kill a hundred cows," the Son of the Leopard said. So they went out to the herds and killed a hundred cows.

"Let us skin them," the Son of the Leopard said. So they skinned them.

They took the skins and softened them. And Wolde Nebri instructed this way: "When the herds are grazing, the warriors will go with them, two men under each skin. When the Halhal come, we shall fight and run away, leaving them the cattle. And when the Halhal sleep, our warriors shall come out from under the skins and slay them."

In three days the Halhal came, seven hundred of them with sharpened spears and leather shields. Two hundred Bora men, Wolde Nebri among them, covered themselves with skins and mingled with the cattle. There was a great battle around the well, and many Halhal and many Bora were slain, and then the Bora fell back and fled.

The Halhal warriors gathered their dead and covered them with stones, then they drove the cattle close to the well and slept. The Bora warriors threw off their cattle skins, and with fierce battle cries they flung themselves upon the sleeping enemy. The Halhal awoke and were confused. They ran this way and that, searching for their weapons, but it was too late. Wolde Nebri was here, there, and everywhere, and his flashing broadsword cut down many a Halhal man in the flower of life. At last the Halhal fled, leaving behind them five hundred corpses, their shields, and their weapons. And those who escaped were caught by the Bora who had been driven away from the well, and they were all destroyed.

The Bora people then celebrated their victory. Their wives and children were brought from hiding, and there was music and dancing.

"Never have we seen the like of this warrior Wolde Nebri!" they said.

And Wolde Nebri said: "I am merely the servant of my destiny."

The metalsmiths of the Bora heated their forges, and made for every man a broadsword like Wolde Nebri's. And he stayed with them until he had shown them how to use this weapon. Then he took his leave of the Bora and went away.

As for the Bora, they marked the blade of every broadsword with the flowering spots of the leopard in memory of the one who had saved them from the Halhal.

The Son of the Leopard went everywhere and sought knowledge. He listened to the sounds of the night, felt the burning heat of the summer sun, felt the torment of hunger, and tasted the flesh of many wild animals. Each thing he scrutinized and remembered. He examined the wild blossoms of unknown trees, saw unnamed rivers rushing away from the mountains, and followed caravan trails through the tall prairie grasses. These things he put away in his mind, but still the knowledge he sought was not there.

He came one day upon a woman crying before her earthen house, and he asked to know the cause of her grief.

"I am alone and live from the milk of my goats," the old woman said. "But there is a great serpent living in the hill who one by one devours my goats, and now there is but a single one remaining."

"Count me as your protector," Wolde Nebri said. "Give me a bowl of milk."

The woman took a silver bowl from her house and filled it with milk from her goat. Wolde Nebri took the bowl to the hill and placed it before the cave of the serpent. The great snake came out to drink, and Wolde Nebri saw that it was as long as ten men and thick as a baobab tree. But he drew his broadsword from the sheath on his back and threw himself upon the serpent,

18

and sought to slay it. And the serpent threw himself at Wolde Nebri and tried to slay him. The battle caused the dust to rise a hundred feet into the air, and the sound of the fighting was heard at the end of the valley ten miles away. Three times the great snake coiled around Wolde Nebri, and three times Wolde Nebri slashed his way free, until at last the monster lay dead upon the ground. Wolde Nebri cut off a piece of the serpent's skin, took the silver bowl, and returned to the house of the old woman.

In gratitude she gave Wolde Nebri the silver bowl. But he said:

"How could I take this bowl? And what need should I have of it?"

The old woman replied: "Take it. In this bowl you will keep the history of your great deeds."

He put the bowl in his leather pouch and went his way. And that night when he sat in a cave before his fire he asked himself how he could put into the bowl the history of his accomplishments. When his fire was out he slept, and the answer came to him in a dream. In the morning he arose and took the bowl and the serpent skin and fashioned a lyre out of them. And then he killed a small antelope, and from its tendons he made strings. When they were dry he strung the lyre, and he played on it and sang:

"Thus it was with the mighty Halhal
When they came by the hundreds with their swords and
*   shields!*
When they came riding and on foot!
When they came to destroy the Bora!
Alas for them, the Son of the Leopard was there!
It does not matter how proud they were!
Their flesh has been eaten by the jackals!
Their bones have been gnawed by the hyenas!
Their wives have no husbands!
Their children have no fathers!
Thus it was with the vain Halhal!"

Each thing he had done he sang about, and in this way the silver bowl held the history of his deeds.

And it happened that Wolde Nebri came one day to the Valley of the Ghosts of the Giants, and he passed through a village of the valley where there was great excitement and confusion. There were many men standing in the center with spears, and in front of the houses the women were talking together.

When Wolde Nebri came among them they accosted him menacingly and asked why he was there and who he was. He replied: "I am he who carries the broadsword on my back. Why do you not say 'Peace,' and why do you not invite me to enter your guesthouse?

Why do you not feed me and bring me water so that I may wash my feet after my journey?"

They asked him: "What are your intentions here? For there is trouble in this village, and we do not know you."

Wolde Nebri said: "I am Wolde Nebri, and I come from the mountain of mountains. This is not my country, and I know nothing of your trouble."

One of them said: "We are of the tribe of Ad Tecles. Last night the men of Za'aw Manatu came and stole for him one of our women."

Wolde Nebri said: "Then why do you stand here? Are you all old men?"

One of them replied: "You are a stranger, and ignorant."

Wolde Nebri said: "I seek knowledge. Tell me."

And they said: "Za'aw Manatu is the last of the race of giants who once lived here. He stands as tall as two spears. He is fierce and violent, and among his followers are a thousand brigands. In this village are only eighty men capable of carrying weapons. Among all the Ad Tecles there are not more than four hundred warriors. How then shall we fight?"

"Let each man carry two spears instead of one," Wolde Nebri said.

An old man came forward and peered into Wolde Nebri's eyes.

"You are young and rash," he said. "It is easy to impale oneself on a spear of the enemy. It is more difficult to live. You must come from a far-off country not to have heard of Za'aw Manatu. He is indestructible."

"I have never heard of these giants you speak of, father. But did I not hear that Za'aw Manatu is the last?"

"Yes, the others have died, only Za'aw Manatu remains."

"If the others have died, these giants are only like the rest of us, who also die. Za'aw Manatu also can die."

"Many have tried to destroy him," the old man said, "and their bones lie bleaching in the sun. For when he was born his destiny was read in a cast of cowry shells. He shall die neither by knife nor spear, neither by sword or club, neither by fire or water. Only by grass may he be destroyed. This is his fate. How then shall we fight? Shall we simply leave our bones in the valley?"

"Forgive me, I was ignorant," Wolde Nebri said.

So they fed him and bathed his feet and put him in the guesthouse, and he lay down to sleep. But he could not sleep because he was tormented by the riddle of Za'aw Manatu's fate. As he lay thinking, some straw from the roof was dislodged by the wind, and it floated down softly and fell upon his chest. He picked it up in his hands and played with it. And suddenly he sprang to his feet and rushed from the guesthouse, calling upon the Ad Tecles to gather. They came and stood before the house, and he said:

"I have solved the riddle. I will destroy Za'aw Manatu."

They asked: "What is the solution?"

Wolde Nebri said: "Send a messenger to Za'aw Manatu, and tell him the one who carries the broadsword will fight him alone in the fields."

They shook their heads in doubt, but they sent a messenger. He was gone two days, and when he returned they gathered to hear what he had to say:

"Za'aw Manatu was angry, and then he was amused. He said: 'Who is the one who carries the broadsword? Any child can carry a broadsword. The man you speak of must be silly and tired of life. I will meet him in the plain. If he kills me you may have the woman back. If he does not kill me I will come and take all your cattle for my trouble.'"

The Ad Tecles listened and they argued: "Why should we lose our cattle also?"

But Wolde Nebri encouraged them, saying: "No man lives who does not die. If I who have nothing to gain have no fear, why do you who have been provoked stand indecisive and trembling?"

They were shamed then, and they agreed.

Wolde Nebri went off in the fields by himself and plucked green stems of grass. When he had gathered a small bundle he went back to the house. He entered and closed the door. From outside they asked: "What are you doing?" From inside he said: "I am weaving."

When the next dawn was breaking the Ad Tecles came to Wolde Nebri's door and said: "We are ready, let us start."

He arose and bathed, and put around his neck his thong pouch, and in it he put the thing that he had woven. Then he joined the Ad Tecles, and together they went to meet Za'aw Manatu.

When they came to the field in the center of the valley, Wolde Nebri saw the army of the enemy in a great horde. Some were on foot and some were on horses, and they all carried spears with many-barbed blades. The Ad Tecles drew up in a line at their edge of the field and listened silently as the enemy shouted ridicule and insults at them.

Wolde Nebri went out to the center of the field, his eyes searching for Za'aw Manatu, but he did not see him, for the man was seated on a rug.

Wolde Nebri called out: "Where is the stealer of women and cattle? Where is the bandit that calls himself a chieftain? Where does he hide and tremble?"

Then Za'aw Manatu rose to his feet, and Wolde

Nebri's tongue fell silent. Za'aw Manatu was as tall as two men. He wore on his head the mane of a lion, and he was clothed in the skin of a kudu. His legs were as thick as tree limbs, and his hands resembled cassava roots. He wore on his shoulder a shield of elephant hide, and he leaned on a battle-ax as tall as Wolde Nebri himself.

To the taunts and insults he had heard, Za'aw Manatu replied: "Where is the girl who makes noises like a man? Where is the cricket who wants to mate with the elephant? Where is the fresh food for the jackals?"

Wolde Nebri said: "Let us see who shall feed the jackals."

So Za'aw Manatu came forward. Before the first blow of the battle was struck, Wolde Nebri took from his pouch the thing he had woven of grass. It was a long and beautiful sling. He placed in it a large and heavy stone. And before Za'aw Manatu was upon him, Wolde Nebri whirled his sling around and around, and discharged the stone from it with a crack like thunder. The stone struck the great Za'aw Manatu above the ear, and he fell on the ground where he stood. Wolde Nebri ran forward with his sword, but Za'aw Manatu was already dead. The bandit chieftain's followers came forward to look. The Ad Tecles came forward to look. He was neither moving nor breathing, and the color of life had gone out of him.

So the bandits took stones and built a mound over the last of the giants where he had fallen, and they delivered back to the Ad Tecles the woman they had stolen from them.

Then Wolde Nebri took up the lyre he had made from the silver bowl, and he gave to it another great deed in its safekeeping.

The Son of the Leopard went back then with the Ad Tecles to the village. There was a great festival celebrating the victory over Za'aw Manatu. They danced all night and refreshed themselves on palm wine. Only when daylight came did they stop. Wolde Nebri went into the guesthouse and lay on his mat, and he fell into a deep sleep. He slept through the day and the following night. And he slept through a second day and night. On the third day he came to the door of the house and said:

"I will settle here among you if I am welcome."

They replied: "You are welcome. You are as one of us. You have given life to our unborn children."

They took him out and put scars on his body like their own. They purified him in smoke, and rubbed his skin with butter. And Wolde Nebri became one with the Ad Tecles. He built a house, and the men roofed it with clean grass. The women and girls came with brooms and swept his earthen floor and the court before his doorway. And there he lived.

Then the old men of the village came to him and said: "This is but half a house."

Wolde Nebri said: "Yes, I have no wife."

They told him: "Why do you not choose?"

Wolde Nebri said: "I will choose."

So he chose a young girl of the village, and the old men went to the house of her parents for him, and it was arranged. On the day that was set, ten young warriors came for Wolde Nebri, carrying their shields and spears. He mounted a horse and went with them to the girl's house, and there they captured her and wrapped her in a white cloth and put her on the horse with Wolde Nebri. They returned to his house, and he carried her inside. And he remained there with her while the warriors drank and feasted before his door.

A time came when Wolde Nebri's child was born. It was a boy. Wolde Nebri went then to the old men and said:

"How shall I know who he is?"

They were perplexed and said: "He is who he is. Give him a name."

"How can I name him until his identity is discovered?" Wolde Nebri said.

"When you name him, then you will know who he is," they replied.

"It was not this way in my village. You are untaught," Wolde Nebri told them. "Isn't there a priest among the Ad Tecles who can divine my son's previous life?"

The Ad Tecles shook their heads. They did not understand him.

Wolde Nebri became angry. He turned his back and left them. He walked through the village out into the open fields. In the distance he saw high jagged mountains standing like a cluster of spears. He remembered then the mountain called Aini and the village called Adi Keritoha. He came to where some children were playing games while their goats grazed. He strode among them fiercely and cried out: "I will play this game also!" But they turned and fled, driving their goats before them.

When Wolde Nebri returned to the village his angry thoughts went around inside him. The Ad Tecles looked at him silently.

It is told that Wolde Nebri soon put his sword on his back, took his lyre on his shoulder and went away without naming his son. But his wife called the child Son of the Broadsword, and so he was known throughout his life.

Wolde Nebri went eastward now, the way he had come, through the country of the Baria, the Habab, the Cunama, and the Tacrura. He went toward the mountains that clustered like spearpoints in the distance. And he came one day to a settlement of the Beni Amer. The men in great numbers were guarding their cattle, and when they saw Wolde Nebri they approached with their shields and their weapons and asked how he fared, and how his family prospered, and when they had finished they asked who he was and what he was looking for in the country of the Beni Amer.

He said: "I am called the Son of the Leopard, and as for the Beni Amer, I regard them as brothers. I cross the grasslands only to arrive at my village on the Mountain of Aini."

So they took him to their houses and fed him and bathed his feet. And they sat together drinking beer made from durra, until after a while they asked him to play on his lyre. Wolde Nebri said not yet, and he drank more beer, and they drank with him. At last they urged him again, and so he took his lyre in his hands to play for them.

Long he sat silent, and his lyre was quiet. He placed his fingers on the strings, but his lyre gave out no music. In his mind he recalled the great deeds he had done, but the words of his songs were sour in his mouth, and he could not sing.

And when they had sat this way for a long while, the chief of the Beni Amer spoke:

"The heart and the lyre are twin brothers. When one grieves the other remains speechless."

Wolde Nebri said: "So it is. How, then, can I play for you?" And he put his lyre aside.

"When I was a child they would not accept me, and they stoned me out of the village, though I had neither robbed nor killed. My only crime was to be the Son of the Leopard."

They asked: "Why do you return?"

He said: "What is a man who has no village to call his home?"

And they said: "If they stoned you before, will they not kill you now?"

Wolde Nebri replied: "I will take with me many men with sharpened blades."

And they asked: "Where will you find them?"

But Wolde Nebri was silent then. At last they took him to the guesthouse, and he slept.

In the morning the chief of the Beni Amer came to him and said: "We have young men in our tribe who will go with you." He called them together before the guesthouse then, and Wolde Nebri counted more than two hundred warriors with weapons.

"May great honor come to the Beni Amer," Wolde Nebri said and he gave to the chief his lyre made of the silver bowl. He stayed with the Beni Amer three days while the men sharpened their spears and their swords and the women prepared food, and then the small army set out for the Mountain of Aini.

When they came to the land of the Bora, the Beni Amer prepared to fight, but Wolde Nebri restrained them. He went alone to the wells where the Bora were preparing to fight the Beni Amer, and they seized him with great shouting and were about to kill him when voices from every side called out: "Stop, he is no Beni Amer, he is the Son of the Leopard." So they let go of him, and his friends among the Bora pressed forward and took hold of his hands. They recounted to all the great battle against the Halhal, and each man held up his broadsword to show where it was marked with the flowering spots of the leopard in memory of the Bora victory.

And when Wolde Nebri had told them where he was going, the Bora gave him three hundred young men with broadswords to go with him.

Thus it was too with the Ad Tecles when they heard where Wolde Nebri was going. They sent three hundred men to join him.

By the time Wolde Nebri came to the Mountain of Aini he had more than a thousand warriors, counting many whom he gathered on the way.

His companions made camp, for the sun was going

down behind the great peaks. They made no fires, so that the enemy would not see smoke and be warned, and they ate their meat raw. And then they took their weapons and began to sharpen them.

But Wolde Nebri could not sit quietly. He took his weapons in his hands and went out from the camp, wandering among the wild game trails of the mountain. He came upon a klipspringer feeding by the trail, and he raised his spear and pursued the animal. The klipspringer leaped among the rocks, but Wolde Nebri's sinews fed on a deep well of anger, and wherever the fleeing animal went he followed.

As they raced along the mountainside they caused loose stones to fall and roll. Sometimes Wolde Nebri was close to the animal, sometimes far away. The sweat came out and ran over his body. The air he breathed throttled him. But still he ran. The jagged rock beneath his feet tore his sandals to shreds, but he did not stop. At last he was close upon the klipspringer and he hurled his spear. Then the animal was gone. Wolde Nebri found his weapon, and he sat on the earth to rest.

And after many minutes, when he rose to go back, he saw sitting before him an old blind man with a staff across his knees. Wolde Nebri would have passed without speaking, but the old man said to him:

"How are your goats and your cattle?"

Wolde Nebri said: "I have no goats and cattle."

The old man said: "How fares your household?"

And Wolde Nebri said: "I have none."

Then said the blind man: "Enter my house in that case. Why do you stand before the threshold?"

Wolde Nebri said to him: "I see no house."

"Are you then blinder than I?" the old man said. "The sky is my roof, the sun is my fire, and I sit upon my hearth."

Wolde Nebri came and sat before him, and shared parched corn from the basket hanging from his shoulder. The old man took cowry shells from a leather pouch and tossed them three times on the ground.

"So they fall," he said. "Each time they fall differently, though they be cast each minute of a lifetime." He felt them with his fingers where they lay. "Each man suffers his destiny, whether he speaks or is silent, whether he rides or walks. Three times you will fail. The first time you will fail through vanity. The second time you will fail through weakness. The third time you will fail through strength. And at last you will succeed through sorrow."

"So be it, father," replied the Son of the Leopard. "May you have years as many as the strands of your beard." And he arose, and went back to where his companions waited, and he slept.

When morning came they sharpened their spears and

their broadswords for the last time, and went up the west trail of Mount Aini. They came to the plain which lay above, and they saw that it was filled with the warriors of Adi Keritoha. They stretched from one end of the valley to another, and every man carried a throwing spear and a round shield of elephant hide. In the front were many who wore lion manes on their heads, in memory of the wild beasts they had slain single-handed.

When he saw them there, blocking his way to the town of Adi Keritoha, Wolde Nebri became hot with anger. And he went forward and shouted insults, saying to them:

"Why are you here, when there is corn-grinding to be done?"

And this aroused the men of Adi Keritoha, for corn-grinding was the work of women and girls. To the warriors of Wolde Nebri they shouted back:

"Why are you here, when there is water to be carried from the well and dung to be gathered for the fires?"

And Wolde Nebri called out in return:

"Go home quickly, lest your husbands find you have left your housework."

In reply the men of Adi Keritoha said:

"Why do you stand quivering like dogs waiting to be kicked?"

The Bora, the Beni Amer, and the Ad Tecles said:

"The men of Adi Keritoha are many and we are few. Why should we fight them?"

The Son of the Leopard replied in anger:

"The lice in their clothes are fewer, but they bite without fear. Are we less than lice?"

So the Bora, the Beni Amer, and the Ad Tecles raised their shields and ran forward into battle. And toward them came running the fighting men of Adi Keritoha. When they met in the plain there was the sound of steel beating on steel and great shouting, and the dust rose from the earth and formed a cloud which hung in the air and dimmed the light of the sun. Of the Bora many men fell, and of the Beni Amer and of the Ad Tecles still more. But Wolde Nebri fought with burning fury, and gave courage to his warriors. The fighting men of Adi Keritoha surged forward seven times, but the eighth time they did not come forward but fell back. And then the Bora, the Beni Amer, and the Ad Tecles gained heart and pursued them across the bodies of the slain. The men of Adi Keritoha turned their backs and fled out of the valley up the trail to the town. Wolde Nebri followed them with his broadsword, striking down stragglers, and with him came many Beni Amer, until at last they were masters of the valley.

First they insulted the corpses of the enemy and stripped them of their weapons. And afterwards they collected the bodies of their own dead companions. The Bora gathered the Bora dead and buried them. The Beni Amer gathered the Beni Amer dead and buried them. The Ad Tecles gathered the Ad Tecles dead and buried them. The Bora bards took out their lutes and sang of their exploits. The Ad Tecles bards sang of the exploits of the Ad Tecles. And the Beni Amer bards sang of the victory of the Beni Amer.

When night came they lighted many fires in the valley and ate and drank beer made from durra. Their drummers played for them and they danced. And at last they fell upon the ground and slept.

Wolde Nebri closed his eyes but his sleep was troubled. The distant cry of the hyena he heard, and the bark of the baboon, so that he was half in the world of sleep and half out. He was neither asleep nor awake, and he lay first on one side and then another. At last he arose and took his weapons and walked in the moonlight, and he did not come back to the camp until the darkness retreated before the rising sun.

The Ad Tecles, the Beni Amer, and the Bora were preparing to journey.

He said to them: "Where are you going?"

And they said: "We have come with you and we have defeated your enemies. We have lost many brothers and cousins. We have destroyed an enemy more numerous than ourselves and caused them to crawl back to their women. But our numbers are not without end, and should the rest of us die our tribes will be deprived of an entire generation."

Wolde Nebri said to them:

"You have been good to me as though we were of the same blood. May you journey in peace. May the hairs of your beards be many. May your cattle multiply. May the poets remember your deeds."

Then his warriors said farewell to Wolde Nebri and went westward the way they had come. Wolde Nebri stood by the ashes of his fire until they had gone, then he too descended the trail to the West.

It is said that he wandered again in the shadows of Mount Aini, and that one day he again saw by the edge of the trail the old man without sight in his eyes, and that the man said to him: "How are your goats and cattle?"

Wolde Nebri replied: "I have none."

The old man said: "How fares your household?"

And Wolde Nebri replied as he had before: "I have none."

The old man said: "Enter my house then, do not stand before the threshold."

Wolde Nebri approached and sat at the old man's feet.

The old man took cowry shells from his leather pouch and tossed them three times upon the ground. He said:

"Though these shells be cast a thousand times on the ground and seem to fall differently, for each man they can tell only one story, and that is his story."

He read the fall of the cowry shells with the tips of his aged fingers, and said:

"The first time you failed through vanity. Yet there are more trials. The second time you will fail through weakness. The third time you will fail through strength. And at last you will succeed through sorrow."

Wolde Nebri spoke to him this way: "Grandfather, what was my vanity?"

And the blind man replied: "Your vanity was blind anger, through which you caused many of your companions to die. They were bound by their promise to fight a battle for you, but you scattered them recklessly and laid waste to their friendship. Blind anger is like a storm without rain. It destroys what lies in its path, but does not quench thirst."

"So be it," the Son of the Leopard said, "I have within me such a storm. Without it where is the meaning of my life?"

"From sorrow will come victory. Find your meaning there," the blind man said.

So Wolde Nebri shared his parched corn with the old man. Then he took his spear, his broadsword, his knife, and his shield and followed the trail which went southward into the country of the Chaha, the Muher, and the Aklil.

✺✦✺

It is said that Wolde Nebri again performed great deeds, and left behind him in many villages the memory of his name and his weapons. And wherever he went they honored him. But at night when he slept he dreamed of Mount Aini and when he awoke he was not rested. At last the old men of the Chaha, the Muher, and the Aklil came to him and said:

"Grandson, you do not rest. What can we do to repay you for the good things you have done for us?"

"Give me men to capture a city," Wolde Nebri said.

They gave him men then, some with horses and some on foot, and he returned toward the town of Adi Keritoha. It took many weeks, for the road was long, and Wolde Nebri pressed them. He made the horsemen go faster, then he urged the men on foot to keep up with the horses. The warriors of the Chaha, the Muher, and the Alkil became lean on the march, and the men and the horses grew footsore. Yet Wolde Nebri grew more and more impatient. He rode forward and backward hurrying his warriors along. And they watched him curiously, for they had never before seen a great hero at war. At last they could see Mount Aini thrusting into the sky, and they said to Wolde Nebri, "Now we must rest."

But Wolde Nebri said: "Now is no time to rest. Rest is for those who have been through the battle."

They replied: "If we do not rest now, we will be blown away by the wind that goes through the pass. If we do not eat now we will not be able to balance our spears."

They made fires then, and ate and slept. But Wolde Nebri did not sleep. He walked among the campfires and the sleeping men and cursed them silently.

"Ah, this is weakness!" he said. "But I will make them strong! I will drive them!"

When day came they went forward again, and by nightfall they were at the foot of Aini. They made camp there, and Wolde Nebri unfolded his plan of battle:

"The warriors of Adi Keritoha are many. They sprout like leaves from the trees. For each of us there are forty of them. We must surprise them. We must strike the town from above."

He led them, not by the roads and the trails, but through the riverbeds and the arroyos. And at midday they came to a flat plain. The warriors were tired, but Wolde Nebri would not let them stop. They saw foam on his lips, and they followed without argument.

As they crossed the flat plain they came upon a group of boys playing shaqui with a ball and sticks. There Wolde Nebri halted. As he watched the boys play, his eyes grew red. And suddenly he ran among them, his spear in hand, shouting:

"I will play! I will play!"

The boys of Adi Keritoha threw down their sticks and ran in terror. The Chaha, the Muher, and the Aklil watched in wonder as Wolde Nebri played shaqui with his good fighting spear. They came closer and heard him shout, "Who will stop me from playing?" He struck at the ball with his spear and cried out childish things. At last he sat down upon the ground and was sullen, speaking to no one. His warriors stood around him and waited. And then the men of Adi Keritoha came swarming down the hillsides into the plain.

The Chaha, the Muher, and the Aklil put Wolde Nebri on his horse. They fled down the mountain by the arroyos and riverbeds, as they had come. When they were at the bottom and no longer pursued, they halted before Wolde Nebri to say good-bye, and they left him.

And this was how the Son of the Leopard failed through weakness.

The people say that Wolde Nebri wandered again, but his heart was no longer in doing great deeds, and the broadsword rusted on his back. He camped without fire, ate his food raw, and slept at night in shallow caves to keep warm. It is said that when the rains came he let them fall upon his head.

When he walked, his eyes were on the ground. When he passed strangers on the road he did not notice them. When he was greeted he did not hear.

Many months he walked, and he did not care where he went.

But it happened one day that he passed a withered old man sitting at the edge of the road. The old man said to him, "Peace," but Wolde Nebri did not hear. Then the old man picked up his harp which lay beside him and began to play. He began to sing of the heroes and the kings of ancient times, and the good or evil they had done to the land, and Wolde Nebri turned and came back. He sat before the old bard and listened, and when at last the song was ended, Wolde Nebri said to him:

"How is your health? And how are your children? And how are your cattle?"

And the old man asked him in return. They talked together, and Wolde Nebri asked if he might pluck the strings of the harp. He took it in his hands and played it gently, and after a while he sang:

"Oh my country, oh my country!
What matters it how many enemy J have slain
When J have no building place for my house?
What does it matter that grain grows in the fields
When the injera is tasteless in my mouth?
Why do the wells give water
That will not quench the dryness of my tongue?"

And he sang again:

"How strange it is that the slayer of the serpent
Has become less than a beggar!
The killer of Za'aw Manatu
Has no perfume for his hair!
The giver of the broadsword
Has dust upon his legs!
The benefactor of the Bora and the Ad Tecles
Has unanointed sores upon his back!"

At last he put his harp on the ground and was finished. The old bard took durra from his pouch and
said, "Eat." And Wolde Nebri ate. He saw then that
the old man's legs were shrivelled and dead.

The old man said: "This happened through knowledge. When I was young I sought the knowledge of
medicine and magic, and I stole a potion from a hakim
of my village. I tasted of it deeply, and when I awak-
ened my legs were lifeless."

Wolde Nebri asked: "Father, did you gain knowledge?"

46

"Yes," the old man said, "I gained it."

"If I had the knowledge I could solve the riddle," Wolde Nebri said. "I too would give my legs for this."

When they finished eating the dried durra, Wolde Nebri took the old man on his back and carried him. In the evening the old man said, "Put me here."

Then he took from his pouch a medicine bundle wrapped in a leaf. Into Wolde Nebri's hand he poured some red powder.

"Here is knowledge," he said, "but taste it gently."

"May the hairs of your beard grow many and long," Wolde Nebri said, and he went away, leaving the ancient bard sleeping by the edge of the road.

When at last Wolde Nebri found a shallow cave, he entered to sleep. But first he tasted of the red powder that was knowledge. He tasted all of it and then he slept.

When he awoke it was still night, but the darkness glowed all around him. He stood up, and found the hard earth soft underneath his feet. When he walked it was without effort, and he seemed to float upward on the trail as though he were on a cloud. When he took his broadsword from his back it was light as a feather. The cold wind that swept through the passes at night was warm and gentle on his skin. He felt neither thirst nor hunger, and time was nothing at all.

The days and nights were all the same. Everything was the color of golden sunrise, and he heard the music of a lyre in his ears.

And then he found himself in the plain of Adi Keritoha. He called out to the men of the town, insulting them with new and unheard-of epithets.

The warriors of Adi Keritoha came down to fight him, but even as they approached Wolde Nebri the golden light around him faded. He felt thirst upon his tongue and hunger in his belly; the warm wind chilled his bones, the sun turned black, and the broadsword became heavy and leaden in his hands.

The warriors of Adi Keritoha saw him fall on the earth, and when he did not rise again or stir they left the plain and went back to their houses in the town, talking about what they had seen.

Night came, but Wolde Nebri lay where he had fallen, as though life had gone out of him. Day came, and at last he awoke.

When he tried to rise his legs would not hold him. They were as two sticks of wood. They felt no pain, neither would they move. At last he understood that he, like the old bard, would henceforth travel only on the backs of horses or men. He sat upon the ground for a long time.

And he remembered then what he had heard in his

youth, that knowledge is strength. And he understood now the meaning of the third riddle.

The people of Adi Keritoha gathered outside the holy mountain cave, while the priests sang and played drums within. Outside, the people talked of what the warriors had seen. They had seen Wolde Nebri, the Son of the Leopard, dancing upon the battlefield, and then they had seen him fall still and dead. The people discussed among themselves whether Wolde Nebri had been slain or whether he had died of his own free will.

One of the warriors said: "He was untouched by a spear. We did not kill him."

Another said: "We did not fight, we only approached to answer his insults."

But an old woman said: "If you insulted him, then you were already in battle."

Inside the cave the Holy Men danced and whirled. First one of them became ecstatic, then another, and a third, until all of them together were leaping into the air stiffly, or hanging to the rock ledges with their fingers, or lying straight and trembling upon the floor. As the dawn came their trances left them, and they sat down together to discuss what they had discovered.

They came to the entrance of the cave and the eldest spoke to the people.

"We heard the words of the Son of the Leopard, for he spoke to us. From his own mouth he has declared we have destroyed him for the second time. His anger is like the wildest mountain storm, and he is preparing to be born again among us. He vows to bring ruin on us, to slay the cattle and burn the fields, to kill all but a single bard who will be destined to wander and tell the story of Wolde Nebri's vengeance."

The elders of the town went elsewhere and talked among themselves. The cattle wandered untended, the men and women did not go down to the fields. And when they were finished the Head Man of the town came back to the people and said:

"Four hundred and seventy-eight years we lived on Mount Aini before the Son of the Leopard found us out. Since that day we have lived in terror and suspense. He has pledged himself to return, and his anger now knows no bounds. We must seek another place for our town, a place without trails on a mountain so high that the birds forsake it."

The people of Adi Keritoha went to their houses and took their possessions. They put the aged and sick on horses or carried them on their backs. They put their millstones on the backs of their oxen. They gathered their cows and their goats from the plains, and they went down the westward trail of Mount Aini. People say that the line was ten miles long, and the dust from the trail rose and hung like a red cloud in the air. It is said that the people of Adi Keritoha passed through the country of the Habab, the Cunama, and the Tacrura. And when at last they had gone through the country of the Ad Temariam and the Bora they disappeared into a wilderness.

The grainfields on Mount Aini dried up, the stone houses were washed away by the rains, and the hot summer winds covered the granaries with sand.

As for Wolde Nebri, a strange thing happened. A wandering herdsman carried him down from the mountain on his back, and left him by a well where people came to water their cattle. He no longer turned his eyes toward Adi Keritoha. People who came to the well brought him injera to eat. And one day a wandering Mensa came with a harp and played at the well. At the sound of it Wolde Nebri's spirit lifted. He borrowed the harp and played upon it and sang. When it was time for the Mensa to go away, Wolde Nebri said:

"Leave me this harp, and take instead my broadsword."

It was agreed between them, and Wolde Nebri felt

peaceful and contented. He played for the people at the well, and they fed him and gave him coins.

A day came when Wolde Nebri left the well. He was carried to the highway on the back of a cattle herder. And again on the highway he was transported wherever he went, either by men or by oxen. He carried the harp with him everywhere, and he sang for his food and his shelter. When the people heard his music they gathered and listened and their spirits were refreshed. He sang the ancient songs of the bards and the heroes. He sang songs of love and nostalgia. He sang of the wild hills and the summer rains. This way the years went by.

And one day as he sat at the edge of a trail he saw a boy leading an aged blind man. He said to the old blind man, "Why do you stand before my door? Enter, and share my fire."

The blind man came and sat beside him. He took from his leather pouch some cowry shells and tossed them upon the earth, feeling them with his fingers.

"Though these shells be cast a thousand times on the ground and seem to fall differently, for each man they can tell only one story, and that is his story," he said.

Wolde Nebri said: "It is the fourth riddle I have never understood. How can there be victory through sorrow? The fourth riddle was not borne out. There was sorrow but no victory. Long ago I abandoned my ambition to avenge myself, and even so the people of Adi Keritoha have fled where I may never follow. Three times the shells were right, for three times I failed, but where is the victory that comes from grief?"

The blind man cast his shells again and again upon the earth, feeling them each time with his aged fingers.

Wolde Nebri took up his harp then and he sang. He sang of the cattle and the peaceful grainfields, of the women who carried water vessels on their backs, and of young men growing into manhood.

The blind man listened and ceased throwing his shells upon the ground.

Wolde Nebri sang of the children of warriors slain defending the village wells. He sang of the trails and roads which wove across the land in every direction, of the metalsmiths and the weapons they made of fine steel, of the makers of leather shields and sandals. And he sang:

"Oh my countrymen!
Why does a man journey forever seeking Destiny?
For Destiny is the companion who holds his hand.
Why does a man search endlessly for a house?
For his heart is the house he lives in."

People who stood by the trail listening to Wolde Nebri said:

54

"Whenever have we heard such singing as this?"

The blind man put the cowry shells back into their leather pouch. And he said to Wolde Nebri:

"Can you sing this way and yet not know the meaning of the riddle? In your song lies the answer. Your victory lies within you."

It is told that Wolde Nebri lived a long life, and that his singing was heard at every watering hole from Cassala in the plains to Berbera on the sea. As the years passed he was no longer known as Wolde Nebri, but as the Brother of the Harp.

This is the legend of the Son of the Leopard. So the old people say.